Tales of a Trickster Guinea Pig

ZORRO
and
QUWI

Rebecca Hickox
pictures by Kim Howard

A Picture Yearling Book

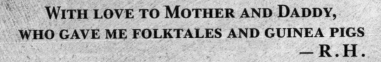

WITH LOVE TO MOTHER AND DADDY,
WHO GAVE ME FOLKTALES AND GUINEA PIGS
— R.H.

FOR MARK AND GRETCHEN SACKETT,
THE BEST GODPARENTS EVER
— K.H.

Published by Bantam Doubleday Dell Books for Young Readers
a division of Bantam Doubleday Dell Publishing Group, Inc.
1540 Broadway, New York, New York 10036

Visit us on the Web!
www.bdd.com

Educators and librarians, visit the
BDD Teacher's Resource Center at
www.bdd.com/teachers

ISBN: 0-440-41183-1
Reprinted by arrangement with Doubleday Books for Young Readers
Printed in the United States of America
September 1998
10 9 8 7 6 5 4 3 2 1

In the mountains of Peru there was once a fox
called Zorro who tried every night to catch Quwi the
guinea pig. Quwi was tired of going hungry while
he hid from Zorro, so one evening he stole into
a garden in the nearby village. Here he could
eat the flowers all night, for
Zorro would not think of
looking for him there.

In the morning, however, the owner of the garden was unhappy.

"*¡Ay caramba!* I must catch this thief before he eats up everything."

That night he set a trap and caught the hungry guinea pig.

Just before the sun rose, who should take a shortcut through this very garden but Zorro.

"Aha!" he cried when he saw the trapped Quwi. "I have hunted for you all night, and here you are, trapped and ready to be my breakfast."

Quwi sighed. "I would be happy to be your breakfast, for something far worse is about to happen."

"What could that be?"

"The owner of this garden is forcing me to marry his daughter. I shall have to live in a fine house, eat rich foods and be waited on hand and foot."

"What is wrong with that?" asked the fox.

"Have you ever seen the girl?" said Quwi. "She's a real beauty, but so much bigger than me! I shall have to be on my guard every minute to keep from being stepped on and killed. I'd rather you just ate me up now and be done with it."

"Let us not be hasty," said Zorro. "What would you say to my taking your place?"

Quwi agreed at once, so Zorro let the guinea pig out of the trap and climbed in himself.

As soon as it was light, the garden's owner, carrying a big stick, came to check his trap.

"So it was Zorro ruining my garden!" he cried, opening the lid and giving the fox a whack.

"Wait, wait!" cried Zorro. "I am here to marry your daughter."

"What!" cried the man, shaking his stick. "Marry my daughter, you say!"

Zorro could see that he had been tricked. He managed to tip the cage and escape, but not before several more lumps were added to his head.

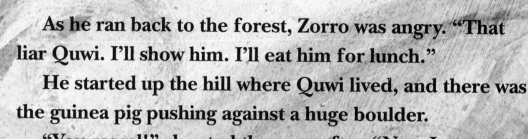

As he ran back to the forest, Zorro was angry. "That liar Quwi. I'll show him. I'll eat him for lunch."

He started up the hill where Quwi lived, and there was the guinea pig pushing against a huge boulder.

"You rascal!" shouted the angry fox. "Now I am hungry *and* sore. I am going to eat you up this instant."

"Zorro, *mi amigo*," answered Quwi, huffing and puffing. "What a stroke of luck that you have come along. This rock was rolling right toward the village. Help me hold it and everyone will cheer us both as heroes."

The vain fox thought this sounded grand.

"Push hard!" warned the guinea pig. "I will go find a wedge and be back in just a minute."

One minute passed, and then two. Zorro pushed as hard as he could, but he was beginning to get very tired. Soon he realized that the tricky guinea pig was not coming back.

With muscles straining, he decided he would have to let go of the rock and jump aside. When he did this, the rock stayed where it was, firmly attached to the hillside.

"*¡Caramba!* Two tricks! He will not fool me again."

The next morning Quwi was digging for tender roots at the edge of a field. He did not see Zorro sneaking up behind him.

"Ha!" cried the fox, grabbing Quwi. "This time I will eat you for sure."

"Go ahead, then," said the guinea pig. "You will have a full stomach, but it won't matter since you will soon be dead."

"What?" said Zorro. "Why will I be dead?"

"*¡Madre de dios!*" exclaimed the guinea pig. "Are you the only one who has not heard? A great rain of fire is coming. It will be here any moment."

"What can we do?" cried the frightened fox.

"Well," said Quwi, "I was digging a hole to hide in. You had better do the same."

Zorro quickly dug a hole and crawled inside. Once the fox was hidden, Quwi gathered several large thornbushes and piled them over the hole.

"Here come the clouds," he called.
"Can you see it getting darker?"

"Yes," said the fox. "Has it started to rain fire yet?"

"It is starting now," cried Quwi, poking the thornbushes into the hole with a stick.

Zorro let out a yelp. "*¡Ay!* The fire rain is hitting me. *¡Ay! ¡Ay!*"

The fox dug deeper into the earth to escape the stinging, then curled up and fell asleep. When he awoke he was very hungry.

"I wonder if it is safe to go out now. The entrance may still be too hot. I will dig a new hole."

When Zorro reached the surface he carefully felt the ground. It was cool. He climbed out, expecting to see a blackened field, but everything looked the same as before. He ran to the other side of the hole.

"Thorns! Quwi has tricked me again, but this will be the last time."

The angry fox searched all day for Quwi, but the cunning guinea pig was careful to stay out of his way. That night, however, Quwi came right to Zorro's den, carrying a little dish.

"Ah, *compadre*," said Quwi, "I feel sorry for tricking you out of so many meals. Here, I have brought you some *mazamorra*."

"This is a very small bowl of sweetened cornmeal," complained Zorro after he licked it clean. "I haven't had dinner yet, and I still think I should eat you up."

"If you won't eat me yet," said Quwi, "I will show you where there is more *mazamorra*."

Zorro followed Quwi through the woods and into the village. Quietly they crept into a house.

"There it is," whispered Quwi, pointing to a clay pot.

Zorro took a little taste just to make sure Quwi was not tricking him, then began to lap up great mouthfuls.

He ate with such greed that in a few minutes he was licking the bottom of the pot, but when he tried to get his head out, it was stuck tight.

"Quwi," he whispered, "can you get me a rock to break this pot?"

"I see one over there," said the guinea pig, "but it is too big for me to lift. Here, I'll lead you to it."

But Quwi did not lead Zorro to a rock. He led him to a sleeping man. The guinea pig placed the fox's paws on the old man's bald head. Zorro tried to lift it.

"¡*Ay! Ay!*" cried the man.

Zorro dropped the man's head. In his fright, he smacked into the wall and broke the jar. When he saw the old man reaching for his gun, Zorro ran through the door, and he did not stop until he reached the far side of the forest.

...g himself a new den and decided ... ...inea pig would be too tough to ...yway.

A NOTE FROM THE AUTHOR

Zorro and Quwi is based on a cycle of tales called
"The Mouse and the Fox" found in *Folktales Told Around the
World* (University of Chicago Press, 1975). According to the
editor, Richard M. Dorson, these stories were told to Jean
MacLaughlin by a thirteen-year-old boy in Arequipa, Peru.
I rewrote four of the episodes, substituting a guinea pig for
the mouse. In Peru, Quwi (whose name is the Quechua
word for guinea pig; in Spanish the word is *cuy*) is the hero
of many trickster tales, although a rabbit or mouse is some-
times used instead. Since I raised guinea pigs as a girl and
now have a daughter who raises and shows them through
her 4H cavy group, I couldn't resist making this personable
(though perhaps not quite so cunning) little creature the
hero.